TUG

A Log Boom's Journey

Scot Ritchie

GROUNDWOOD BOOKS
HOUSE OF ANANSI PRESS
TORONTO / BERKELEY

I'm helping Dad on the tugboat. We're going to tow a log boom to the sawmill on the river.

The boom boat pushes the logs in place. Then the deckhand uses his pike pole to pull them together. He's making the log boom. The logs around the outside of the boom are chained together.

Dad hooks the steel cable to the
log boom, and we're ready to tow.

I look out for ferries and other boats in the harbor. We steer wide around a tanker.

When we go under the Lions Gate Bridge, I hear a clap of thunder. It starts to rain.

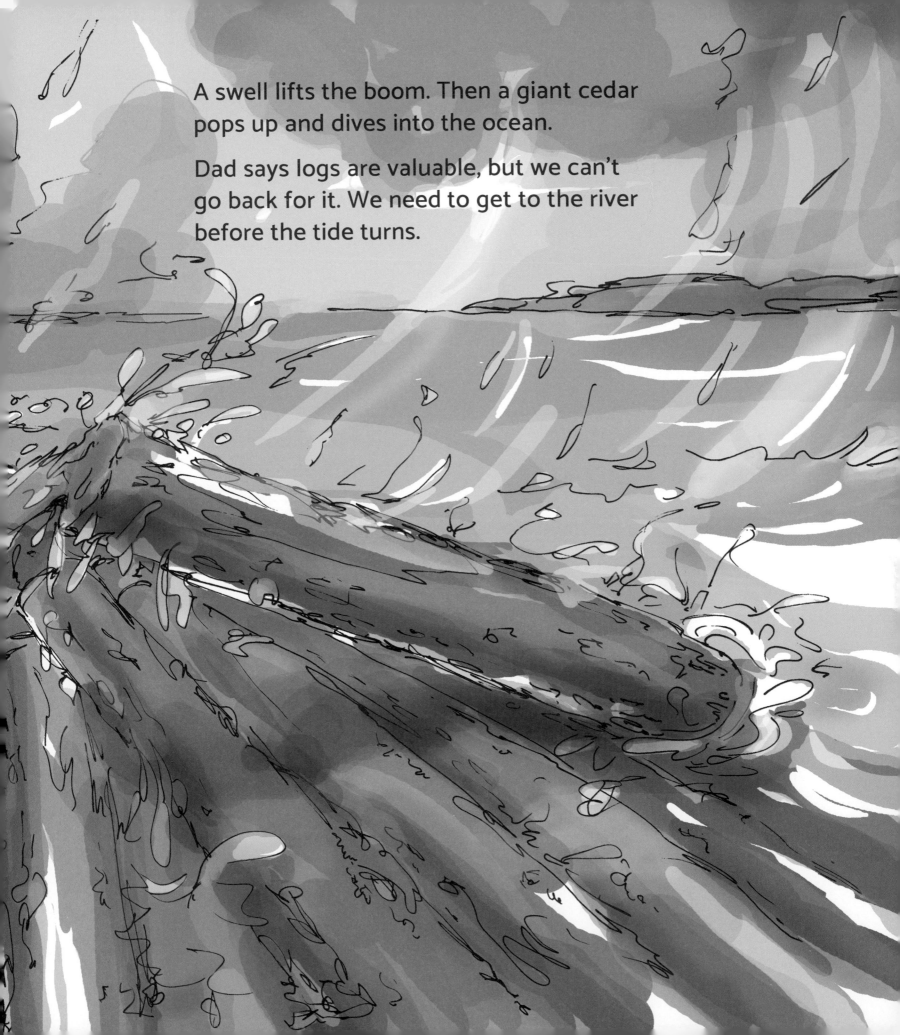

A swell lifts the boom. Then a giant cedar pops up and dives into the ocean.

Dad says logs are valuable, but we can't go back for it. We need to get to the river before the tide turns.

I can already see a beachcomber. He's spotted the log.

He claims it by hammering a dog line into one end.

Finders keepers!

We reach the river just in time. When the tide turns, anything that isn't anchored or tied up will be pulled out to sea.

Dad shortens the tow line as the riverbanks close in.

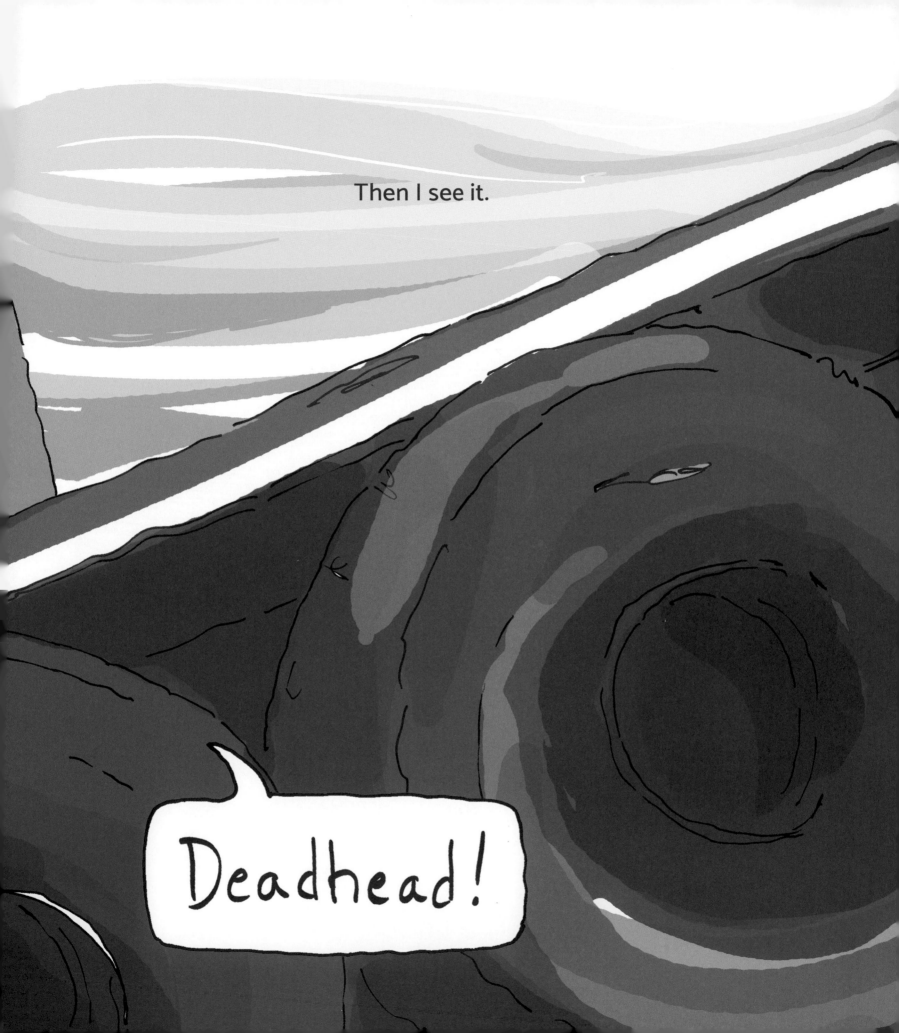

Dad cuts the engine and
grabs the pike pole.
He pushes it into the log.

Then he hammers a spike into the deadhead so we can tow it to the mill.

A deadhead is mostly underwater. You can run into one without even seeing it.

We're drifting, and so is the log boom.
Dad starts the engine, and we chug ahead.

The wind blows, and the smell of the sea is gone. Now I smell the sawmill.

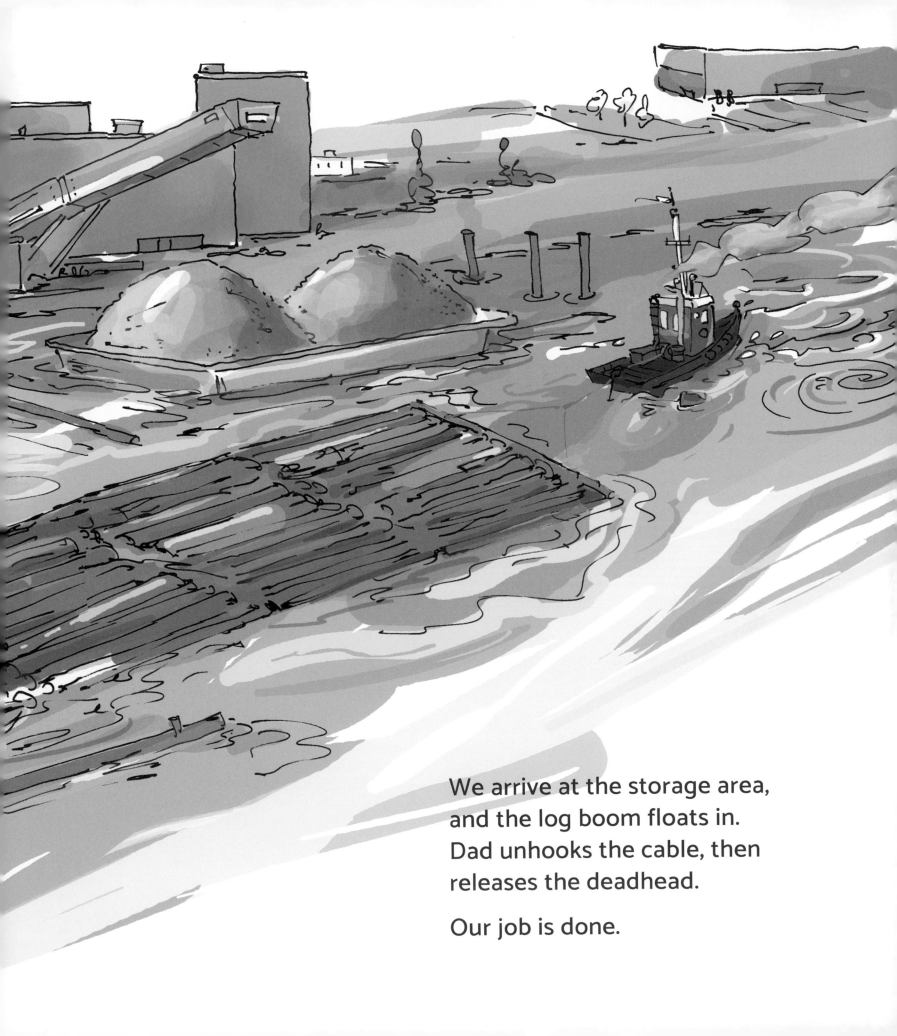

We arrive at the storage area, and the log boom floats in. Dad unhooks the cable, then releases the deadhead.

Our job is done.

Maybe I'll drive the tug one day.

Glossary

Beachcomber – a person who earns money collecting logs found at sea or on the beach.

Boom boat – a small boat used to sort and push logs together to make a log boom. It is driven by the boom-boat operator.

Boom sticks – the logs around the outside of the boom that are chained together to keep all the logs inside.

Deadhead – a partly submerged log, with just the top visible.

Deckhand – a person who works with the captain, making and securing log booms with tools such as pike poles and boom chains.

Dog line – a rope going from a boat to something else, like a log.

Log boom – a collection of floating logs, for towing or storage.

Pike pole – a pole used to push or hook onto something, often a log, so it can be moved.

Sawmill – a place where logs are cut into lumber.

Swifter wire – a strong cable, or wire rope, that helps hold the boom together.

Timber mark – the branding on a log, used to identify it.

Tugboat – a boat used to pull or push large ships, cargo or logs.

Dear Reader,

Growing up on the West Coast, I would stand on the beach and watch mighty little tugboats tow log booms many times their size. One tugboat can tow thousands of logs! *Tug* is inspired by those days, when it was common to see log booms in Burrard Inlet, off the coast of Vancouver, British Columbia.

Logging often takes place deep in the forest where there are no roads. A single logging road is built so the logs can be trucked to the ocean (or river), then floated to their destination. If there is no water nearby, the logs are moved by truck or train, or sometimes even by helicopter. But water transport is easier and better for the environment. The tug in this story tows a boom of logs from the forest to a mill where they will be cut into lumber.

Long before commercial logging began on the West Coast, First Nations people used and cared for the forests. In less than two hundred years, logging on Traditional Territories has changed the forests significantly. Now we know we must take more care to conserve the forests, but how we manage them and improve logging practices are discussions that continue. Indigenous and non-Indigenous communities, governments, and people working in forestry and logging are asking: What is our role in reducing climate change? Can logging be sustainable and done with care and respect? How do we maintain healthy forest ecosystems for future generations?

I don't have the answers to these questions, but I know that how, where and what kinds of trees we log will change. For now, I still go to the beach and watch the tugboats. Some tow log booms or huge barges, others help large ships position themselves at the dock. If you come to the West Coast, why not wave to the captain when you see a tugboat chug by?

Scot Ritchie
Vancouver, British Columbia

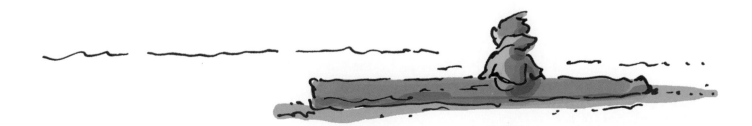

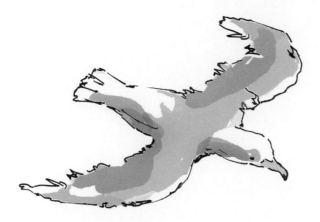

To Rick Smith, who worked in the woods and on the water. Thanks for your stories and knowledge.

Text and illustrations copyright © 2022 by Scot Ritchie

The publisher would like to thank Dr. Gary Bull of the Department of Forest Resources Management at the University of British Columbia for reviewing the text and illustrations.

Published in 2022 by Groundwood Books / House of Anansi Press
groundwoodbooks.com

Groundwood Books respectfully acknowledges that the land on which we operate is the Traditional Territory of many Nations, including the Anishinabeg, the Wendat and the Haudenosaunee. It is also the Treaty Lands of the Mississaugas of the Credit.

We gratefully acknowledge for their financial support of our publishing program the Canada Council for the Arts, the Ontario Arts Council and the Government of Canada.

Library and Archives Canada Cataloguing in Publication
Title: Tug : a log boom's journey / Scot Ritchie.
Names: Ritchie, Scot, author, illustrator.
Identifiers: Canadiana (print) 20210234504 | Canadiana (ebook) 20210234598 | ISBN 9781773061771 (hardcover) | ISBN 9781773064307 (EPUB) | ISBN 9781773064314 (Kindle)
Classification: LCC PS8635.I825 T84 2022 | DDC jC813/.6—dc23

The illustrations were first drawn in pencil, followed by line work in ink. They were then scanned into the computer and colored in Photoshop.
Design by Michael Solomon
Printed and bound in China

The Log Boom: A Close Look

Swifter wire

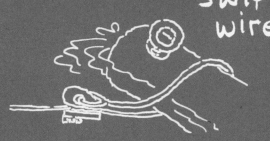

Ring   Toggle

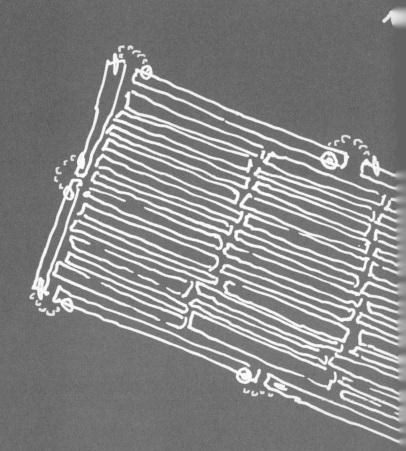

Chain

Timber marking